THE SPUD

Published by
*f*eatherproo*f* books
Chicago, Illinois
www.featherproof.com

First edition
10 9 8 7 6 5 4 3 2 1

Library of Congress Control Number: 2018942679
ISBN: 978-1-943888-16-0

Edited by: Tim Kinsella
Proofread by: Sam Axelrod
Cover illustration by: Tiia Lindström
Design by: Tiia Lindström

Printed in Canada
Set in Crimson Text and Ostrich Sans

featherproof BOOKS

IDAHO STATE HWY 33

crashes happen when a person gets hit by remembering, kp decides, sitting in his truck at the wheel with a dorito and a baseball cap, foot on the brake. his brother walks across the parking lot.

today's a damned day, his brother says, a piece of cardboard floating in the sky.

it's not about you, he explains one night on the patio with his feet up like he's about to be filmed for the movie's extras edition while kp turns into the lot. and it's not about me. his brother unwraps a toothpick. it's about damning the damned, kp hears somewhere between parking his truck and opening the grocery store door, holding five boxes and a clipboard.

B&B GROCER

a girl in a rain jacket sits in front of the store. eats candy fish, calls herself jd. darlin, you can't love one, one. she tears off a fish head, talking the song, can't love one and still have fun i'm leaving on the midnight train oh gee, i jim, wutta wutta wut a man. she buries the yellow plastic in the dirt. darlin, you can't love two, two. a truck pulls up and parks. can't love two and still be true i'm leaving on the midnight train oh gee i jim, wutta wutta wut, her tongue sweeps the back corners of her teeth, a man.

sitting on the curb, she watches herself in a scene from her morning shower, water traveling thick across her face. it's been eleven months now, she says, fingers like smooth forks through her hair. i call it love cause it doesn't leave. the small dark seeds on her face are freckles. she hopes they still look dark like that now, sitting on the curb. i could go anywhere and everything would be related to it, she says, squeezing water from the bottom of her strands. i mean, i don't wanna be you, she says, the soap out.

she sits in front of the grocery store in her rain jacket with a backpack and a gun. a man walking to his car says sun's a real nickel today huh, on his phone. big dumb sky, she personally says, but he doesn't ask. it's been three minutes since kp walked inside with a clipboard and some boxes, she counts, wearing his cap.

83422

this is where the boxes go.
i'm stealing you.
uh.
i'm stealing you.

36 S. MAIN ST

a girl runs and jumps into the truck bed with her two legs that open exactly the second he looks, probably tenth, maybe eleventh grade legs not accompanied by anyone but a woman's forty year old stare telling her to get out of that car. he's working, and this is not the right place to go for a run. neither kp nor the woman ask if she's okay. what would they say? are you okay? what would that do? they don't have a first-aid kit. they don't know her song.

this is where the boxes go, kp says to her, holding his truck keys and a deliverUS clipboard. he's cleaned out the tones in his voice so that no sound can be traced to a specific time, place, or person, jd notes. it's been nine months since their first real conversation, she counts, ten since she first heard about his brother and she stood in front of kp in line at b&b grocer figuring out what exactly she could say to him at this moment in their overlapping lives. what's in minestrone? she decides. water and vegetables, kp says, the consonants of his voice splintering. this is where the boxes go, he says now, each sound straitjacketed. it's sad to see him, standing over his voice, strapping it down.

i'm stealing you, jd says, holding the gun to kp's face. nice not to hear his brother's explanations, just a girl in his car, giving demands. i'm stealing you, jd repeats, alone, in her shower.

BROULIM'S

several months after the initial formation of damning the damned and a year before his brother kills twelve people outside a bakery in driggs, kp wins a state-sponsored hot dog eating competition. he sits on a raised platform behind a table and eats 26 hot dogs in ten minutes. his brother takes a picture of him standing with their dad. i can't say i'm proud, his dad says before the shot.

now kp's deleting the picture on his phone, convincing himself the rain jacket girl might steal it and send it to the teton daily for some kind of inspection. that's the thing about dying, his brother explains, kp seeing them eating in a pizzeria suspended somewhere in whites and reds, anthony wearing his xtract shirt. people should know by now! anthony says, slurping his straw around.

the clerk at the store holds the clipboard in his hands, signs and starts a smile, but kp looks away when he introduces the eyes. to say we're only standing here to do the delivery, so give the clipboard back.

83422

so what's your favorite problem?
my favorite problem?
yeah.
i don't really do that.
lungs, for me. or phones.

5000 S. HWY 33

jd sits in the passenger seat of the truck, gun like a metal shoe in her lap. they've been driving for ten minutes, and, although jd has "stolen" kp, he's driving to his next delivery job at rexburg gas. then airport, then glass, few after that, the one in ketchum, and then back.

it isn't horrible to have her company, kp decides. she doesn't play music, she doesn't take pictures with her phone, and although she laughs without explanation and occasionally squeezes the inside of her tenth grade thigh in a way that makes him ashamed to be sitting next to her in a private vehicle, kp watches a lot of comforting images when she speaks – images he left in houses and schools and cars, ones that might be helpful in a lighter future, like arranging grapes as a face on his dinner plate with his dad and helping the pretty tall girl in his eighth grade science class memorize lip shapes from the common face shapes chart in the lab. of course there are other images he sees that he immediately scratches out with the imaginary black sharpie he and his aunt label THE HAMMER one morning at her breakfast table, aunt gwen calling this process "an introduction to modern medicine," but he feels so familiar with the hammering medicine these days and so far from the months with his aunt, that the best tool right now is a detached eye, watching everything pass.

jd looks out the window. the tetons are giant brown blobs that dip into the sky. she points her gun at them from behind the window glass. blobby parasites, damning the sky. hearing anthony make this conclusion instead of her, pressing the gun tip to the skin valley in her neck. she likes resting the gun there. feels like all of them are going to sleep, in a desert, somewhere.

PENDL'S

at 10:44 a.m. on the morning of the attack, anthony paxton is stopped at a traffic light 0.3 mi outside of the bakery, where kp now sits with jd, waiting for the green. he was eating a hard-boiled egg, recalls nearby driver harriet volokh in a fifty second video clip kp watches the day after on his computer screen. kp recognizes the woman from the idaho dmv, grey bangs and a mole on her cheek. he was dropping shells out the window, volokh explains. i told him there was a garbage can right down the block where he could put those shells. anthony responded: thanks. nine minutes later, he shoots and kills twelve people, and then himself.

83440

24

i saw you in my gym class once.
your gym class? when was that.
i think you knew my teacher.
your gym teacher?
your brother came too.
what were we doing there?
i don't know, you were there.
ok. what's your teacher's name?
mr. mercery. he was in dtd.
oh yeah, jesse, ok.
did he help start it?
start what?
dtd.
oh. no.
did you?
i don't know.

TETON HIGH

the track's pink and huge. a big pink circle beneath the mountains, like someone was trying to add some color in the deserted rock scene but got tired and let the dust win. she's walking it. thinking what did i do wrong that i am here with these people and their phones and their eyeliner on this wannabe pink wiped off round thing with a clock testing how many minutes it takes to run a mile.

this is jd's favorite scene. she's seen it hundreds of times, now watching it in the passenger seat with the gun in her lap. first she's walking the track, looking at the tetons, it's awful etcetera etcetera, then she decides to check if mr. mercery is going to tell her she needs to at least do the walk-run, "you're being lazy," "you used to run it in eight minutes" –mr. mercery, a heroin addict or something that makes you skinny and gives you fork bites on your arms, who used to coach her in soccer until she quit (no one else ever scored), who her mom once said had down's syndrome as if it was 100% fact at the royal wolf with the larthrops and no one knew what she was talking about. so she looks over at mr. mercery but he's not watching anyone in the class. he's talking to two boys.

what kind of pink is this? one of the boys asks as jd finishes her last lap. he has a cloud-shaped birthmark on his neck, the prettiest brown. looks like stale fucking laundry, he says, and then turns to her. don't you think so?

REXBURG GAS

kp pulls into the spot, unbuckles. another truck next to him, a man in a camouflage hat carrying sprite and beef jerky to his car. jd sits cross-legged in the passenger seat, the gun in her lap. i have to go in, kp says and she nods and goes with him, to get more gum.

five deliveries left for the day and now this girl. kp carries a box around the store to the back, AC27711 on the white tape, flipping through scenes for the circle of her face or her freckles on the road, a friend standing next to her, holding a can at a race, maybe those striped shoelaces in the wolf lot, her lips on the creamery swirl, index finger with the ring adjusting her strap near the cone, but none. she's buying gum in the store, so she has money, so maybe she bought it, didn't steal it or take it from home, maybe she just bought the gun and likes him, so that's why she's come along.

he's in the driver's seat and she's still inside, probably in the bathroom, tying up her hair or looking in the mirror, so he has a minute, and her backpack's on the seat. he watches his fingers pinch the zipper, then a loud slide.

there's too many people, you know? no one needs you. it's not like there's any holes in the universe that develop when you leave, where you used to exist. you're supposed to die. even stars die, they die and turn into dwarfs that shatter into giant balls of dust, and no one in the galaxy approaches a little piece of dust and says, "we missed you, star!" -you're not exactly supposed to live- so it's only natural that people would start killing each other and then forgetting about it. it's not sad, it's not.

IDAHO STATE HWY 20

her mother peels an orange at the dining room table. they don't talk. all scenes with her look like this, jd decides, cracking her knuckles in the passenger seat of kp's car.

she writes on a piece of paper at her mom's table. things she needs to do: cut hair, put up picture, cover up the lazy eye on her skateboard. why she hasn't turned in homework for ms. whitney: she had a math test and math is hard (has no emotion) and english is easy (if you know talking) so she figured she could make the papers up before christmas break, since she's already read the books and knows what to write in the corner in red. but what to say if she saw damning the damned in the downstairs bathroom? not mine, mom. it's not mine.

her face a deflated pillow, once pumped with tight goose feather, now sunk. i'm just concerned, her mom says, peeling the orange at the table. should i report you? they both sit skinny, her mom placing orange triangles in her glass. out the window of kp's car is a wendy's sign. jd watches her hair turn red, into two pig-tails, sitting across from her mom with the bucked tooths wendy smile. i just don't know, julia, her mom says, scooting in her chair, picking up another skin triangle. i just don't know.

231 S. HWY 33

today's an especially damned day, anthony says to five other boys. people die and i should know that by now, but i guess i don't. he's standing at a wooden podium in the spud's drive-in parking lot while the boys drink beer and soda. you walk around with these pigs in your ears and then you come home ready for a meal and your dad is dead and your brother's sitting there like he's eaten fish legs –they look at each other –but people die. kp looks at the ground. cement. i should know that by now.

kp sits on a toilet seat in idaho falls, listening to the audio on his phone. his brother's unusually serious here, like the actor decided to play him flat-faced and sad, picking kp to be the main audience, not aware he'd be facing a piss-stained wall inhaling his own dorito shit while making the assessment. one seat, one sink. like most gas station bathrooms in the state. like most jail cells in the country. it's funny, kp decides and flushes. or sad.

he soaps his hands. we need him to cooperate with us or we're more likely to assume he's an accomplice to his brother's murders, one teton police officer says to the other, standing in kp's kitchen like a beige piece of cardboard while kp stares at him from the couch. two talking cardboards next to the refrigerator, breathing fan sounds. he lived in this house, he attended the DTD meeting every month, and yet, he's claiming not to have any involvement? kp looks at his hand on the couch. now under the faucet. not cardboard, but close.

83401

lets stop. i'm hungry.
i have to deliver these boxes.
you don't have to. no one's boss.
i know a good place to eat in pocatello.
do you even know my name?
no, cause you didn't say.
well do you want to?
sure, okay.
it's jd.
jd?
yeah, like yours.
not really. mine's kp.
yeah, they sound the same.

he has the same freckles. the only thing she likes about her face, and now, on someone else.

she sits on the grass by the track, pretending to watch the sky, the inside of her better ear directed toward the t-shirted boy, taking in the climate of his words: “traveling insect salesmen,” “elevator shove,” “to no one’s own” –realizing her brain had been arranged in neat, rectangle drawers, and this guy, he can take it out. he probably doesn’t even have a drawer in his house.

sitting on the passenger side, finally. eleven months since the day they met. the girl has always been a big part of It, she hears someone intelligent in a newsboy cap tell the reporter when he asks. she was celebrating the anniversary of her release from the american box, another intelligent person with a bowtie will add, and mr. mercery will say, yea, she was always super fast, and her mother will go through the comforters and blankets in jd’s room, looking for a note, late for her dance class, wondering where her daughter is, jd always making her late to her dance class, that silly dumb-haired girl who hasn’t even kissed anyone and is almost sixteen years old, but there won't be any note for her mom, nope. just a souvenir from DTD and a bowl of old cereal.

231 S. HWY 33

anthony sits on the ground, peeling an orange in the parking lot. thanks, jesse, he says after listening to jesse's fifteen-minute description of eating ribs on the school bus with jeremy latch.

kp's watching another spud scene in the driver's seat, listening to jd tell a story about her coach (jesse) bringing a pistol to soccer practice so they'd run extra fast. it wasn't loaded, but jesse said it was, which is why kp's rewinding to the parking lot, looking at jesse's smile. it's a smile kp never noticed until now, sitting in his car with this teenager and her gun. only corner teeth in the smile, the beginning of a spitting or a gargle. something jesse only wore to DTD meetings, probably. on a date with a beautiful girl he wouldn't wear it, on an airplane, no, in class, no, in his jail cell, maybe. does anyone else have a dream they want to tell? anthony asks, sitting on his knees in the dirt, placing another orange piece in his mouth. the actor plays him sweet in this one.

reporters arrive at kp's house an hour after the shooting. where were you? they ask. did you see your brother this morning? what time? what was your brother doing? did he say anything? who else lives here? what about you? got a dream to tell?

83401

i like this flavor gum.
me too.
is it raspberry?
i'm not sure.
i like raspberries.
me too.

IDAHO STATE HWY 20

a construction site of cut down trees roped off in a square, prepping for christmas, the lone pines with white bags over their heads, trunk legs sticking out like suffocated, plastic-headed children, a morgue in the daylight, kp decides, as a telephone wire slices through the sky.

THE BIRTHPLACE OF TELEVISION a sign says in front of a one-story house, a cob-webbed stack of wood in the yard. my mom took me here once, jd says, pointing at the house. is everything birthed? she asks her mom as they walk past the sign and ring the doorbell. be polite, julia, her mother says, wearing a long red coat with symmetrical buttons. be polite.

i hate tv, jd says now, staring at a man driving a tractor through the field. THERE IS EVIDENCE FOR GOD, a billboard says with a child held by his mom, jd sliding her fingers across the gun.

DIXIE'S

kp orders grilled cheese and coke. jd orders chili in a large piece of bread, shaped like a bowl. they don't talk. there are three other groups in the restaurant. a wrinkly, hunched over couple looking at their forks, a man too big for the booth, wearing old buckles, and a girl with her mother, talking about chicken bone. the clock is a circle above the entrance and says it's two in the afternoon. it's two in the afternoon on a wednesday in a diner in idaho falls and kp's drinking soda with a girl whose pretty pretty, but young.

i don't believe in hierarchy, jd says as if someone has asked. she has the same kind of anthony speak, kp notes, watching his brother's mouth smooth apart the hierarchy word on the patio while kp accidentally burns his arm with a cigarette. it's all the same. people, places, words, germs. me and you, we're all the same. his brother's words aged, scenes mixing; the death feeling old.

kp decides not to look at jd anymore, the temperature of his hands heating as he watches her mouth get tight and full around the spoon. he forces his attention off her mouth and on the nearest shoe.

83401

your dad died, right?
yeah.
did you cry?
um.
sorry.
it's fine.
no, it's a bad question.
it's okay, i didn't cry.
you didn't?
no.

DAVE'S

anthony paxton comes with his then-girlfriend, lauralie cooke, the evening before the attack. the local bar is 0.9 miles away from the location of the morning shooting, four blocks parallel to main street, the voice explains to non-locals while kp bites into a chicken finger on the way to his aunt's house. the bartender (tim), an old friend of anthony's, says the 23 yr old killer bought ms. cooke one teton ale, and nothing for himself. kp squeezes barbeque sauce out of the packet and onto his chicken. he had this idea about being sober. knowing yourself in every condition, tim says as kp pulls a long strand of hair out of his mouth. there were four other people at the bar, not including paxton and ms. cooke, says the voice, a voice that sounds like it's from arkansas. she loved him a lot, a new voice says. it's rosie, lauralie's best friend. kp turns up the volume. you know the kind of love when everything's blurry beside it? rosie's family is mormon. she paints. it's like a big planet you live on, with no one else.

they sit at the bar for two hours, kp learns while parking his truck on the front grass of his aunt's house, waiting for lauralie's comment.

the voice says lauralie drinks a teton ale, while anthony orders nothing but water with ice. you always wanted to hear what anthony was saying, rosie explains. lauralie doesn't comment.

kp looks at jd's head against the window. hair tucked, potato brown. like anthony's, not lauralie. but now i see it clear. he was just sick. rosie says, just a sick boy, and different from everyone else.

50

the dolly has five boxes on it, moving across the airport carpet like a toy car with a forty-pound hat.

kp guides it, keeping the wheels on the flat line. jd wanted to follow him inside, but he said no, and she said yes, and he said you can't get a gun past the security guy and she said fine. so she's waiting at his truck, probably eating candy or doing ballet, but he took his keys so she can't steal his truck. he has two more deliveries and she doesn't want to go home. why, he could ask. cause i'm stealing you, she says in her close-up.

i'm stealing you, her lips say, outlining slow. she's not wearing anything, but it's cut off past the neck. i want you. her lips, a sliver of nose. box, box, box, this is a box. take me, a black bra strap appears in the frame, and her small, pretty finger walks across her neck. cardboard box, you're in an airport with a cardboard box, cardboard box. she closes her eyes and leans her head back. no longer cut past the neck. kp, the naked girl whispers, suspended somewhere in whites and reds. her eyes are closed, finger circling her breast. kp, she says, the circles getting small. kp, bad, he says, box on the floor, THE HAMMER out.

83274

take your feet off the dashboard.
okay, no need to get all pissy.
well this is my truck.
yeah, but i have the gun.
well shoot me, then.
you dare me?
no.

IDAHO STATE HWY 15

there are no mailboxes on the highway, jd notes, but there's one other car on the road. the other, plus them makes two chunky metals following one yellow line. the yellow line's the leader and follows the pavement, who follows the sky. all damned to each other, jd quotes, collecting pieces of anthony's sayings about stealing mail and the perils of paved roads. she shades a leaf in her notebook with a pencil.

i almost had to fire anthony when i realized that, the manager of the sporting store says, hands on the hips of his bike shorts. jd's watching the scene from the car, where she's studying an anthony video on her laptop, wearing a pajama shirt that says SWEAT + SACRIFICE = SUCCESS in a red white and blue soccer ball and wishes she was wearing her bad brains shirt or her ussr trench, holding two pump shotguns, or a 9 mm carbine, one for the camera, one for the head, but oh well. another guy says the stealing mail stuff was not part of DTD. she writes this down.

the paxton brothers, jd learns from the clip and rewrites on a new page of her notebook in kp's car beneath the burger challenge schedule, were caught by their father, who is not alive. according to mag hartley, who has an annoying potatohead accent and makes peanut brittle every sunday with her mom, the dad did not bring his sons to the police but had them formally apologize to each person they hurt. "the boys came over and knocked on my door," mag says, pointing to the big oak door jd opens sometimes. anthony spoke first. he stepped forward and said: ms. hartley, on the account of me and kp, i really do apologize for stealing your mail. we were curious, that's all. mag shakes her head. just awful. just awe-full, jd says.

jd's book is anthony's book. her gun is anthony's gun. her hair is anthony's hair, her words are anthony's words. like an actress playing the teenage girl version, kp decides, watching her choose and memorize sentences and then scribble them out, cross-legged and serious, so serious she looks silly, holding that gun. things are funny because they're damned, anthony says during their first DTD meeting while kp eats a snickers next to his friend, sam. sam doesn't talk to him anymore. he goes to college. the two of them chew with their mouths open, watching anthony from their seats on the ground. and things are damned cause they're funny. anthony says, double dimpled smile, makeshift stand.

did you ever come to DTD meetings? kp asks, unable to stop rewinding. rewinding, and for what.

she comes to the last one, jd says, but hides in the small delapitagated barn thing that used to be the spud movie theatre. none of the boys see her, but she hears anthony speak about no thingness and she hears mr. mercery laugh. she also hears a girl's voice say he's joking, right? – talking about anthony, who is all loud with no thingness talk. jd peeks out the side of the movie barnshack to look at the girl. lauralie, soft.

83221

do you like driving?
yeah, it's okay.
it's like inside, but outside.
well mostly inside, but yeah.
my mom won't let me drive.
because you're too young?
no, cause i might crash.
you think you'll crash?
yeah. of course.

GLASS & CO

the repair shop is a fenced up rectangle, across the street from a dog kennel. kp drives to the boarded front entrance, checking his clipboard in case he's made a mistake. auto glass services, 2235 garrett way, idaho falls, 83213. he squints to see the number. no mistake. a yellow note saying WE ARE OPEN.

he's not tempted to steal peoples' mail anymore. if he was still eleven year old kp, (and maybe he is, just plus eight years, ten inches, and a dead dad and brother) he might open one of the envelopes to see what's inside, maybe a rock from italy or some letter that says please leave and come to my house where we can swim and eat grapes or go for a walk. the envelope is exciting cause it keeps our images inside, anthony says, sitting on a log at the creek, holding three envelopes for mag hartley. hopefully opening them doesn't suck. he hands one to kp, the first of dozens that summer, riding bikes. dear taxpayer, kp reads out loud, –no. it says taxpayer? anthony asks, not believing, taking the letter back, looking for a name, still scrawny here, wearing the same basketball shorts as kp. we considered form 8857 and are prepared to deny your claim. this letter is not a denial of your claim, but if you do not respond to this letter within 30 days, we will send you a letter denying your claim. that, and an address.

kp walks inside the repair shop with his clipboard and gives it to the man. are you mr. d'agastino? he asks, hoping for a second he'll say yes, i am, and sound like rome. but he says no, and his voice is a clear idaho.

83201

you look familiar.
oh yeah?
you live in pocatello?
no, driggs.
oh! driggs.
but i deliver all over.
maybe that's it.
i have two boxes for you.
oki doke.

crash is a movie, and a word, and usually involves cars or bikes or people bumping their heads. it's used to describe a person who's called steady, and then falls, or a person who has a lot of energy, and then none. the person crashes. people crash every day, he knows, driving, seeing crash crash crash. does he want to crash? no, and he never did, but this girl, with the gun. she does, and so did his brother. another nihilist, mike murdow called him in the times: cool. casual. kp reads, standing in the bathroom of a sandwich place. do we have a good argument against these people? murdow asks, hot coffee and scones and twelve people dead, with no answer. kp looks at the girl. dead, more people. and he'll say what.

IDAHO STATE HWY 20

there are more cars with canoes and dogs as they get closer to ketchum, kp's last delivery for the day. both front windows are down, not much wind, just tetons and sky and jd dropping her wrappers onto the highway. she clicks as they drop. shoot and play once, and never again. kp takes the gun.

what are you two gonna do in ketchum? kp's dad asks, sipping coffee out of the gracy's mug, reading his teton daily as white light slices through a window behind him, leaving one eyebrow in the shade. kp looks for his baseball cap, the same grey hawks one he wears now next to jd in the car, punching him in the arm, trying to steal back her gun. i don't know, dad, kp says, his body so small it disappears behind the couch as he crouches down.

anthony comes down the stairs, hair wet, sticking up from the shower. i wanna see where hemingway shot himself, anthony tells their dad, playing a gross heartthrob today, all sunned and freckled, shirtless. huh. well do you want to see where hemingway shot himself? his dad asks kp, and kp shrugs. like in most scenes, his performance is dull. well what am i supposed to do? kp says, turning off the highway, to unload the gun.

83215

you're such a fucker.
i'm a fucker, you're right.
you could've helped.

CRATERS OF THE MOON PRESERVE

the visitor center is a brick square on a hill. a sign has three red arrows pointing in opposite directions. dry lava under sky. they turn right, toward BROKEN TOP on the basalt.

you know what a phreatic eruption is? kp asks as they drive around the purplish-blue rocks. she shakes her head, no eye contact. it's when hot lava touches water and explodes. he points to a pile of rocks. like those, he says, memorizing a diagram in his textbook on the back patio while anthony twists back lauralie's arms, stohhp, she says, smiling, kp pretending not to watch. stop, the word cut off by a rough breath, really –now choking on the letters, arms beginning to spaz, stoh–, anthony laughing, tickling harder, her eyes accelerate towards kp, suddenly horrified, make him stop. the windshield, a purple rock. is corbo still at the school? kp asks, refocusing on lines in the teacher's cheeks, his bald spot. jd won't look, drawing circles on the window with her finger. he was a good guy.

they drive into the orchard, a group of lava-transported cinder cone fragments, frozen plums. kp stops the car. the sky is the brightest grey. jd bends down and picks up a rock. puts it in her pocket, next to her knife.

IDAHO STATE HWY 20

both sides of the valley are wetter and greener than the potato flats. an old phone booth and a white van in one of the fields, a kids' superman cape waving and tied to the phone booth like the state flag. cottonwoods and two long telephone wires, the CONOCO GAS sign.

this is how you play predator, anthony tells kp on the floor of their living room one night while their dad makes enchiladas in the kitchen. if you get less than nine energy points you die and come back to life as the next animal down the food chain. kp nods, bent over his knees on the carpet. humans and sharks are at the top and can eat everyone and destroy anything, anthony says as his dad sweeps behind him.

a boy's mouth wide open for a scream or a dentist chair on a billboard. WHAT DOES METH DO TO YOUR BRAIN? the sign asks, the boy's face turning into the fourteen year old face of his brother, sitting on the floor, playing predator, mad and discolored from losing all his energy points and forced to become a plant. then a gun to his head, and a shot. kp loosens his fist on the wheel.

83320

you like applebees?
like the restaurant?
yeah, we just passed a sign.
my mom makes me go sometimes.
that's cool. she takes you out and stuff.
kinda lazy, actually. sorta insulting.

jd plugs her phone into the radio wire. a rectangle on her thigh, making a black halo. kp watches it vibrate, a tongue getting electrocuted as it turns on.

she's naked, pink little nipples out and pointed in the passenger seat with her legs open, heels pressed into the dashboard. she slides her rolled-up rain jacket between her thighs. fuck me, she says, just fuck me. she leans into his shoulder, come on, her nipple hard against his arm. do it while you're driving, she smiles, wrapping her rain jacket around his neck. he takes his hands off the wheel and lets the car slide, wandering into the other lane as they crash and cum.

images can get violent, aunt gwen explains, stirring scrambled eggs over the stove while kp sits at the table, hard grey pockets under his eyes. he revisits this scene when he needs to. he'd probably still be watching porn and letting aunt gwen get drunk every day if it weren't for the hundreds of times he's replayed it – aunt gwen telling him how to use THE HAMMER, drinking a mimosa at three p.m. while he sits at the table adjusting his eyelids to the daylight after five hours of naughty teens getting cream-pied on his computer screen, the mimosa glowing like a nightclub sign in her glass. when an image leads you somewhere violent, take this, she says, holding a black sharpie in her non-mimosa hand. and scratch it out. she scribbles in the air. kp looks at his hands on the steering wheel. jd draws in her journal next to him, fully clothed.

231 S. HWY 33

jd walks across the gas station parking lot, opening her new pepsi bottle. she drinks. it's the same plastic container kp bought every day in high school, the container he used for his dip spit, water, gum. jd opens the passenger door and gets back in. you look like a robot, she says, and rolls her window down.

a sports car accelerates past them, shaking the seats in kp's truck. zero bullets in her gun now. you gotta stop drinking this shit, anthony tells lauralie on the phone while ladling red sauce onto dough. kp listens, elbows on the counter, eating crust. no customers at the pizzeria, and when no one's there, anthony calls lauralie. kp likes that he can't hear her responses. it lets him imagine her voice, and her imagined voice gives him soft instructions for the day.

why are you just sitting there? jd asks, kp now seeing the position of his body, hands under his thighs, shoulders unusually strict, and instructs himself to remove his hands, to put the right one in his pocket, the left one on the wheel, take out the keys, turn the second bigger one into the ignition, and reverse out of the lot.

83333

76

this is kech-95 and that was let it bleed.
the harsher version of let it be.
asking for coke and sympathy.
just a space in the parking lot.
great song or overrated, phil?
i dunno, but one of his best.

jd drinks soda and listens. the radio, the radio, kp tries to focus on the word, on the rrrs and the air behind the windshield instead of the voice sound, narrating another crash.

two days after the attack, kp's found at the old drive-in movie theatre, sitting on the ground. police take him into custody for what police sgt. davis describes as "suspicious suicidal behavior." on the ride home from the police station, kp listens to the radio voices talk about teton county. we're receiving a lot more suicide calls, a lower-pitched voice says, naming himself hotline director. the suicide rate in teton county increased from an average of 3.8 per year to 12.2 per year, the hotline director says. we've had more calls within the last year than in the entire 23-year history of our organization. suicide calls like wonderful sweaters for the fall, kp decides, wondering if they receive the same amount of murder-suicide calls, if they consider murder-suicide calls in their studies, if murder-suicide is a word in the dictionary now, if the employees at the suicide group are friends, if they call each other to rehearse explanations, if one of them got the job because once, he made a call.

and just a reminder to our listeners, mountain lifestyles is having back to school discounts until next sunday, so get on over there, people! jd caps the bottle and turns the radio off.

the image & the perception of the image exist in the same image but they differ in their systems of reference, jd reads from a page in her notebook. she rests it on her knees in kp's car. this is cause the perception is selective in its system and only keeps part of the image and subtracts whatever doesn't interest it. the perception exists on its own system, a double system of reference. kp parks on the main street of town while two men in cowboy hats with fishing rods walk past the car. the perception is submissive in the image universe, but it's also selective. jd watches a man stub out a cigarette on the ground. it chooses the content.

jd sits at her desk at home, mapping out her plan. she reads anthony's online notebook for damning the damned, published after his death by a former member. she writes most of the words down. a lot of jokes and references to russian and french philosophers, explanations for the meaning of the word damned, the meaning of the word revolution, family, nation, a venn diagram of guns versus nuclear war, stick figures of americans holding small square stick telephones, standing on pits of fire, hair and hands in cartoons of dead breakfasts and populated events in the state, pros and cons of the carbine, a pencil drawing of anthony's dad sitting in a chair with black crosses over his eyes, detailed analyses on national security procedures vs wartime procedures vs peacetime procedures vs prison cell routines vs bedroom blueprint layouts.

do you want to come out with me? kp asks jd from the window, holding his clipboard and a box in front of the americINN sign. she doesn't respond. a small truck selling corn across the street beneath an oak tree reads: soon will be gone.

83333

welcome to the americINN, is this for us?
yep, just this one box, and a signature.
and how are you doing today, sir?
alright, thanks, how are you doing?
i woke up with this bruise on my neck.
oh yeah? how do you figure that happened.
must've lost a fight in one of my dreams last night.
oh huh, dang. does it hurt when you put pressure on it?
yeah, even iced it this morning, with my coffee.
oh, i'm sorry to hear that. maybe ice it again?
yeah, you're right. you want a cup? coffee.
oh sure, that'd be great. thank you.

IDAHO STATE HWY 75

they have an indoor pool? jd asks as kp closes the door to his side. fun. she points her sharp little knife at his heart. the sun in the window frames her hairline in a soft gold. kp closes his eyes, tired. you can give me back my gun now.

name, place of birth, height, weight, social security number, are you the actual transferee of the firearm listed? are you under indictment for a felony, are you a fugitive from justice, an unlawful user of marijuana or any depressant, stimulant or narcotic drug? have you ever been adjudicated mentally defective, are you subject to a court order restraining you from harassing, stalking or threatening your child? who writes this? anthony asks, filling out a white form at s+s sporting store while a man tries on wool socks and kp stands in the corner, pinching the inside of a bulletproof vest.

kp hands the gun to jd. it looks like anthony's. jd unzips her backpack and takes out a plastic bag of gold bullets. she loads them into her hand, then into the gun. anthony and kp walk to their truck. what are you loading it for? kp asks his brother, two years ago, opening the car door. don't do that, kp tells jd now. she smiles.

COLLEGE OF SOUTHERN IDAHO

the town of hailey has the sawtooth national forest, red devil peak (6594 ft), della (6729 ft), the rotarun ski area, two bmx parks, and a sun valley polo club building. a golden eagle with his hands on his hips on the sign, the bird wearing a big t-shirt reading CSI.

anthony paxton was an orphan, the dean says into a microphone, standing in front of a crowd in the university auditorium. he had no support here. no allegiances. kp looks at the faces in the chairs, some nodding, but most still, like cardboard circles of faces glued onto couch pillows, the pillows molded into shapes of torsos, arms and necks. kp recognizes one of the cardboards as a mother. he's seen her twice since the shooting. she's always soft and purple. once she looked at him and blinked, like she was going to sleep in the street, and he ought to leave her alone, to rest.

jd's hair flies around the window as they pass the college campus, gun clenched in her right hand near the door handle. he had no support. no allegiances, the dean says at the podium a couple weeks after the bakery. kp pulls his cap further down on his face, doesn't want eyes to meet eyes. he wants to leave, but the people will see him and they'll think he's awful. for leaving, for coming, for listening, for not asking his brother about it, for not making him lose his keys in the morning, for not having smart, beautiful, meaningful things to say to him over dinner. kp closes his eyes beneath the cap, above the wheel. in the dark, he sees himself walking up to the mom after the speech. he's tall, she's soft. neither of them speak. he holds her, and the other people walk out.

83330

has the back to school bigfoot burger challenge started yet?
lotta folks are here, but the contest begins at four.
about how many people are there right now?
maybe fifty. are you a ticket-holder, ma'am?
yes i am. are there many seats left or?
most people are sitting on the grass.
and are there camera-men there?
cameras are allowed, uh huh.
and news reporters?
oh sure, some.

IDAHO STATE HWY 75

the girl's standing in front of the peak, talking on her cell phone, gun shaping her back pocket into a triangular square. kp parked in the driver's seat, watching her, like the scene where the girl calls her boss to complain about the sky, too blue, too big, too bland, and her boss, a big time tijuana drug dealer says he's on his way to meet her in his fat yellow hummer with a trunk full of guns, girls and cocaine. jd puts her hands in her front pockets, arches back to stretch, the perfect ass, small and firm and sixteen years old, all by itself, standing so classically upright in the faded blue as the gun rod presses on the cheek, the arch slowly ripping open the center jean seam, the ass bare, in his hands, on his lap, his pants down, dick out.

THE HAMMER can replace porn for you, aunt gwen explains on the back patio of her house, drinking a club orange cocktail out of her bozeman horse mug as kp takes off his cap and cracks knuckles one by one in the mitt of his hand. are you even ejaculating anymore? or is it just numb now, aunt gwen asks, the afternoon light dimming the comet-shaped scar on her jaw. you can black out all those images, k-p babe, they're separate from you. they don't belong.

jd closes the car door. fuck mountains, she says, kp summoning his aunt's black sharpie to scratch out her thighs and the thumb between her lips, all the dripp milk color to leave only the flat interstate, so-called, between idaho and what, idaho and what, a red ticker passing fifty, sixty, seventy as the girl in the passenger seat peels off her socks.

existence is not only in the realm of humans, which means an identity is not necessarily a person. a person has a face and a body, but these parts are not the identity. the person tells herself what she is. jd studies anthony's words in her notebook. she reads them in a whisper, by the window, as if reciting numbers that open the one and only members united key to the steel prison door, a door bolted shut by laws, suspended over a lamely bubbling ocean, housing the adrenaline and persuasion of the boy and his damning elevations, her casual, t-shirted killer, holding the knob in his palm. the telling makes the identity. the telling makes the existence into some thing sensical, some thing historical, but it's not. it isn't some thing; there is no thing, no thing to look for, no self to find, only the jerk of a laugh. jd relocates her eyes onto the man next to her, looking for a fraction of the related hero beneath the cap, in his blue jumpsuit or square patch deliverUS red and white marking on the breast – looking for a brother, or not.

this is the gripe booth, anthony explains to the small crowd in the parking lot, standing next to a magazine stand and an open suitcase, a snake circle of wire and microphone laid out. jd watches through a slice of wood in the hut next to the seated boys. it records only garbage, anthony says, smiling his famous double dimpled smile, the one jd cut out of the newspaper and glued into the back of her notebook, the one kp scratched out. stole it from the pioneer house.

did they arrest you when your brother killed all those people? jd asks, sketching a bobble-headed dictator in her notebook. bet they were scared of you, she says, bottom lip lazy and lingering, anthony style.

they didn't arrest me. they asked me questions.
like was he working alone or with a group or?
was he showing any signs of schizophrenia, was he on drugs.
because they think no sane person would ever kill people, huh.
it's against his whole thing to romanticize someone, you know.
i'm not romanticizing him; i just happen to agree with him.
but he went against all his main ideas in the end.
no, he just finally took all his words seriously.
he didn't believe in seriousness though.
exactly. it's a joke. a killer joke.

RICO'S

the ketchum sign isn't falling over now. and there's no man smoking all cocky and cowboy against the pizzeria window, and there's no girl in the car. kp's in her seat, anthony driving, anthony talking, his song playing, warm and august in the valley, kp tries to feel, but his skin won't let him, his skin clings tight to itself in a freezer where the girl keeps walking in, asking is this where he shot himself? i want to see where he shot himself, twirling the gun around, drawings of her dictators on the internet the next day, that hot t-shirted teen body on the pavement leaking purple blood from a fresh hole above her earring, clenching the gun in his scratched out, sharpied, tool-filled and now emptied freezer, this left-fanged child, planning futures of failed lungs, forest fires, and baby north koreas for an otherwise just okay couple sharing afternoon slices of pizza, dead and damned to repeat, like any good slogan, dead and damned, at the wheel, picking up her gun, his brother saying yup, smiling, this is exactly where it happened, as they pass the sign, two years ago.

83201 IT'S NOT ABOUT YOU 83330 I'D RATHER WHAT 83422 TWELVE PEOPLE DEAD 83320 NO, I MET YOU IN GYM CLASS 83422 YEAH JUST SIGN HERE 83221 FUCK ME, KP, FUCK ME 83422 SURE, HE'LL 83422 AND YOU JUST WATCHED HIM FILL THIS OUT AND YOU FIGURED WHAT 83221 SO A PROFESSIONAL THEN 83274 IT ACTUALLY SAYS THAT? 82301 OR PHONES 83422 THIS IS WHERE THE BOXES GO 83422 I'M STEALING YOU 83215 WELL I WOKE UP WITH THIS BRUISE ON MY NECK 83333 DO YOU ALSO 83333 LIKE A BIG PLANET YOU LIVE ON, WITH NO ONE ELSE 83330 THAT BIRTHMARK 83320 WELL I SAW YOU IN GYM CLASS 83422 AT THE SPUD 83422 IT'S FUNNY 83422 WELCOME TO DAMNING THE DAMNED 83221 IT HAS TO BE THAT ONE 83422 DAMNING THE DAMNED 83330 TRASH 83221 YES, GRIPE THAT'S THE WORD 83330 JUST TRASH 83221 IMAGES CAN GET VIOLENT 83274 DO YOU EVEN EJACULATE ANYMORE 83221 ALMOST HAD TO FIRE HIM 83274 BUT AREN'T YOU RELATED 83201 FUCK ME, KP, JUST FUCK ME 83215 DO IT WITH YR SEATBELT ON 83215 JUST FUCK ME 83422 SURE, HE'LL

foot on the brake, where chevy meets pole, chest meets rock, pillow in neck, bigger than the girl, the white bags, over the heads, two people, all people

83340

102

repeat after me.

after me. after me.
this is the disaster response unit.

231 S. HWY. 33

nine year old lilillie sits on top of the tractor chewing a sour straw. she chews loud like a baby cow with an eating impediment and bowl shaped hair, big cow eyes fixated on the man in front, turning a shrub into a swan with his scissor hands. her eyes don't leave him, whose blue-lipped face fills the screen, propped up thirty feet by large metal rods, invisible to her, making the screen look like a floating billboard in her family's galaxy of stars. lilillie places another candy in her mouth. her friend hoists himself over the upper window of the tractor, arm tucked and careful not to spill the kernel top fluff in his paper baggie of popcorn. they're the only people on a tractor there and maybe the only kids not old enough to be smoking paul halls and playing never have i ever on the spud's back field, but they prefer it this way. how red is my tongue? lilillie asks him, opening her mouth just enough to see the beginning of her tastebuds. like faded red. not real red, not not red, kp says, sitting on the back of his knees beside her. how many popcorns do you think you can fit in your mouth? he asks, not paying attention to the screen, which has zero girls on it. nineteen, lilillie says, as if the number is go, green light to start their stuffing, kernels filling up the cheeks, a crowd filing into the room of the mouth, stuffed cheeks, on the screen, the billboard.

IDAHO STATE HWY 75

kp lays on a mattress in the bed of aunt gwen's dodge, a stuffed piggie on his elbow. the wind's warm and his aunt's singing something, kp notices as he sits up, trying to place the song along her hairline, swaying under a ribbon. kp? she says, seeing kp now in her rectangle mirror. how you feel?

a thick white tape wrapped around his head, a cloth that keeps the red from dripping.

kp looks at the mattress. a queen or a full, sheetless, taking up the whole bed, the only car on the road, summer wind, his aunt singing cheer up sleepy jean, oh what can it mean, horns coming in, to daydream or believe, hair in ribbon, ribbon in hair, oh what can it mean, cheer up sleepy jean.

83340

excuse us, miss? miss?
what? i wasn't driving.
this is a deliverUS truck.
okay, i'm not the driver.
we can deliver the last box.
okay, i'm not the driver.
are you okay, miss?
i'm fine, this is fine.
do you need a ride?

RICO'S

two men selling soap. hatted and suited in beige lavenders, their holsters hold soap bars next to guns. red and white snap-photo dots circle the head behind them. halo or no halo.

jd sits at a table with plastic chairs. she's waiting, keeping a straight back, not playing with the pepper shaker, not crossing her hands. this is a pizzeria, she repeats to herself, you can slouch a little, but do not play with the pepper, the parmesan, the salt, your hair. this is a pizzeria. the man behind the register looks at her. she holds a piece of paper in her hands. i'd like to work here, she says, before.

one of the soap salesmen holds a sicilian in front of his face. my pizza mask, he says, and the other man laughs, cutting his pizza with a tiny knife and fork and tiny hands. jd forgets to nod, noticing the absence of soap on his badge. maybe he's pretend soap and really military or pretend military and really delivery. maybe, she says, and closes her eyes.

IDAHO STATE HIGHWAY 20

kp and lilillie leave the spud tractor and kiss in the field. it's dark and kp says lilillie's face is a good moon, full, lighting all the people, and they walk to his house. lilillie does not become a hopeful neutrogena and does not move to california, she stays in driggs and works at the creamery and makes a chocolate malt for kp after school every day and comes over to eat dinner with his family and holds his hand under the table while his dad and anthony talk about the construction of the colosseum. she tells them a story about a stuffed crocodile called monstermonster (by the "beach people," anthony has heard of them) and how one afternoon the crocodile opens his mouth and shows them he's missing all his teeth, and the people laugh. she talks to anthony the night before pendl's, late outside the barn while he smokes a cigarette that he does not smoke and she tells him she "gets it" but don't you wanna stick around and see? don't you wanna stay and see? yr just another stuffed crocodile like me and we've got a lot of good company here in the kitchen, and sure there's not really a point but all the smells, all this cooking is the point.

in that movie, jd is lillilie and kp is kp and jesse is anthony and anthony is the dad and the dad's alive.

the people at the bakery die but it's okay because they wipe off the blood and stand up. like kp, in the bed of the truck. looks like you're feeling better back there, aunt gwen says in a perfect lililliee accent. but the sky is no stuffed crocodile, and there's no monstermonster nearby.

83440

gotta stay awake, kid.
just five minutes.
dangerous sleeping.
just five minutes.
yr concussed, kid.
just five minutes.
we did the delivery.

4226 TILTON ST.

one-story. rug, cardboard boxes, a seat near a microwave with a revolving bowl of smart-mac cheese. aunt gwen stands in front of the microwave, her left hip popped slight against the counter, the bone doesn't fit. everybody is throwing out their microwaves these days, she says as the bowl goes around.

jesse and kp sit at the table. jesse's hair all pieced and wet from walking nine miles in the rain back from jail, no phone number to call, holding out his thumb on the side of i-75, three quarters in his pocket. people don't pick people up, he says in the passenger seat of her dodge, but who cares. nine miles is nothing, he says at the table, spooning pieces of yellow cheese into his mouth.

is anyone hiring, do you guys know? jesse asks as aunt gwen pours herself a glass of water and sits on the couch. maybe the movie theatre, she says. they're always hiring.

the camera's not in the picture, but it's working now. she knows because of the flash against the t-shirted boy's burger, mayonnaise dripping down the side of the patty as he bites, bigger than his face, two hands clenching bread, a swallow. the soap salesmen stand on both sides of jd as she watches.

this is how you escape from handcuffs, anthony tells jd one night, holding a sharp knife and a potato in the kitchen of her mother's house while her mom tends to the barbeque outside. do you know what SPUD stands for? he asks, unlocking the cuffs around jd's hands with the tip of the knife. the society for the prevention of an unwholesome diet, anthony says, and jd wakes up and tries to go back.

people used to think potatoes shouldn't be eaten, jd says to herself, watching one french fry enter the mouth of a man and another one fly into the air, beneath a cloud. they had to use a narrow spade to dig up the roots and since the plant lived so deep in the ground, it was considered dirty food. the soap salesmen watch the six men slide potatoes into their mouth.

83452

116

you plucked all your eyelashes off, huh.
well just the right eye. i didn't mean to.
does it hurt, or what's the blinking like.
this eye versus the other one?
yeah, is there a difference.
probably. i don't feel it.

460 E. HARPER

too tall for the tub, has to hyper-extend her legs and go all the way under, feet against the wall. at least they're high arches, jd decides. guess that's a pretty part –the curve before the heel. pretty, but not warm. doesn't even fit in the water. julia? her mother's voice pale on the other side of the door. do you want your dinner in the bathtub?

you don't even have clothes to wear tomorrow, jd says, sitting on the toilet in a trench coat, cigarette tucked under a fat lip, two fingers curved over the gun. the perfect haircut. brown and short and piecy, like every girl in a badly beautiful stance. you can't go to school, are you kidding? that cut isn't even cool looking, it's ugly. she looks at julia, extended in the tub. you can't just go back.

hands pressed toward the ceiling. yeah, the inside corners of her eyes clench against a water bead, i know. the towel folds too still on the floor, but everyone's alone, a water bead lodges itself in her lower lash, so. she studies the ceiling tiles for a face, a nod, a neck – only paint, chipping, and a stain near the pipe. can you just give me something? she asks, the bead releasing itself from her lash, down her cheek. just something.

GRAND TARGHEE RESORT

the steel cable loops around a cushioned bench. fixed grip, kp notices, sitting next to the guy who always compliments his bike, in their shorts on the lift, ascending to the height of the trees. kp takes off his baseball cap, smoothing over the sweat sculpting the hair around the bandage. beautiful day, huh, the guy says, recapping his flask, as if the sky appeared to him only now, after a sip and a rest. i love august.

the front tire hops over a log and turns past a skull sized rock. good reflexes, his dad says on the walk home from his little league game. that's what makes you a great shortstop. kp nods, noticing the width of his dad's arm beneath the shirt compared to his own – half of half. gripping the front bar as the bike speeds under a long branch, an umbrella curling into itself, the guy who always compliments –behind.

wanna go again tomorrow? another sip from the flask in the driver seat window as kp hoists his bike into the back of the dodge. i gotta work, kp says, and his dad closes the latch.

83422

what about the glorious revolution.
well it was bloodless, right? 1688, king james.
mhm... a transfer of power without any blood.
isn't it also when two-party politics begins? at first.
where are you getting that from, julia? in the text?
it just seems like it set that precedent.
um, well, we'll come back to that.

can only circle around a number so many times before it becomes just another line and texture for the thumb, jd decides, standing at her locker, unable to land exactly on the three, always two or four or an extra circle behind.

but the thing opens and it's empty and she puts her chemistry book inside. keeps the ap history one in the pack since ms. maclean was dumb about the new world motivational stuff today and wants them to write the indentured servant's letter for tomorrow.

is that a DTD picture??? a bright oval, this grey eye. not too blue, not too laundry. i always wanted one but didn't know where to get it delivered, the girl says, the gap between her front teeth letting in the perfect amount of dark. tall, coated, french, california. it's sick! the girl says, her tongue releasing the end of the word into soft, pointed splinters. i want.

THE CREAMERY

white's not a shade, it's a color the kid's picking out. vanilla or mint, maybe both. tetons upside down in the long rectangles, dots of sky on the kid's shirt, a sunned man looking for a quarter in his pocket. kp sits at the wheel, the light still red, and there's the girl. standing behind the counter, wearing his cap.

i just need a napkin.
one or two?
one's fine.

kp
jd
anthony
whit paxton
lauralie cooke
jesse mercery
mrs donata
aunt gwen

kp
jd
anthony
whit paxton
lauralie cooke
jesse merccry
mrs donata
aunt gwen